FISHMONGER

AND

WORDSMITH

Fishmonger and Wordsmith

FRIENDSHIP STORIES

Kristina Drake

First paperback edition January 2024

Book design by Kristina Drake
Illustrations by Kristina Drake

ISBN 978-1-7382211-0-3

Published by Cat Creek
www.kristinadrake.ca

For my dear friend FC —

May we always have days like these

Quiet

Fishmonger sat at her kitchen table. She looked out the window and watched two yellow birds at the birdfeeder.

Fishmonger sipped her coffee. It was hot in her mouth, and the mug was warm in her hands. The sun coming through the window felt good on her face. She closed her eyes and tilted her face toward the sun beam.

The two birds flitted and fluttered about the birdfeeder. Then they flew off.

Wordsmith knocked lightly on the door and went in. She was sweaty and a little out of breath. She had pedalled her bike up the road to see if Fishmonger was home. Wordsmith put a brown paper bag on the kitchen table. Inside the bag were

two croissants. Fishmonger poured coffee into a mug for Wordsmith.

Fishmonger and Wordsmith sat at the table and looked out the window. The two yellow birds were back at the bird feeder.

Wordsmith and Fishmonger sipped their coffees. They ate the croissants. Crumbs fell on the table. They pushed the crumbs into little piles. They sipped their coffees again. They looked out the window.

Fishmonger said, "It's nice and quiet."

Wordsmith said nothing at all. She only smiled.

Tired

"Fishmonger!" cried Wordsmith, "what are you doing?"

Fishmonger was sitting on the floor of the *poissonnerie*. She sat with her knees pulled up to her chest and her arms wrapped around them. Her chin rested on her knees.

Fishmonger shrugged and didn't look up.

"Fishmonger, you don't look well," said Wordsmith. "Did something happen?"

There was a half-cleaned fish on the counter, with Fishmonger's filleting knife beside it. Many more fish to be cleaned filled a bucket on the floor, next to the table.

The room smelled like fish, and the air was humid and warm. Fishmonger was sitting on the mucky floor. Something was smeared on her forehead and in her hair and on her clothes. Wordsmith thought it looked like fish guts.

Fishmonger looked up with only her eyes.

"Fishmonger, are you hurt?" asked Wordsmith.

Fishmonger shook her head "no."

"Why are you sitting on the floor?" asked Wordsmith.

The poissonnerie floor was not a nice place to sit. Fishmonger went to the poissonnerie to stand at the counter and prepare fish. She never went to the poissonnerie to sit on the floor. Wordsmith thought something must be very wrong with her friend.

"There's too much fish," said Fishmonger.

"It's true," said Wordsmith, "you have a big bucket of fish to clean and sell at the market tomorrow."

"I'm so tired of cleaning fish," said Fishmonger.

Wordsmith sat down on the floor next to her fish-covered friend. "Yes," she said, "cleaning fish is a lot of work. Is your knife well sharpened?"

Fishmonger shrugged.

"May I sharpen it for you?" asked Wordsmith.

"I'm tired of fish," said Fishmonger.

"Ooooh, I see," said Wordsmith, "you're *that* kind of tired."

Wordsmith sighed and thought about what to do. Her friend was sad. Wordsmith looked around the poissonnerie. There were no windows. A bare bulb on the ceiling lit up the room.

"Fishmonger," said Wordsmith, "it is a

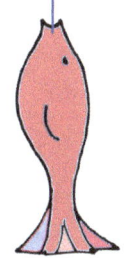

beautiful sunny day outside. The birds are singing. Maybe you need to see the sunshine and the birds."

Fishmonger shook her head "no." She sat very glumly. Wordsmith put her arm around Fishmonger. They sat together in the muck on the floor.

"I need to clean fish," said Fishmonger. "But I don't want to."

Wordsmith thought for a moment. She wanted to help her friend feel less glum. "I can clean some of the fish," she said.

Fishmonger shrugged. Wordsmith saw that this was a very stubborn glum.

Fishmonger said, "I don't want to be a fishmonger."

"Ooooooh," said Wordsmith.

"I am a bat scientist," said Fishmonger.

"Oooooh," said Wordsmith, again. "It's true," said Wordsmith thoughtfully, "you are a bat

scientist. You also make very
tasty fish. The people at the market love
your fish. It makes them happy. And you earn
money with your tasty fish."

Fishmonger only shrugged.

Wordsmith said, "I am a
wordsmith and I make money from
writing words. I don't always like the words I write.
Sometimes I don't like being a wordsmith. I would
much rather be a great poet."

Fishmonger turned to look at Wordsmith. She
wore a puzzled expression. "I thought you liked
being a wordsmith," said Fishmonger.

"Sometimes I do, and sometimes I don't," said
Wordsmith. "But today, I will be a fishmonger. I
won't be as good as you, but I will help you prepare
the fish."

Fishmonger shook her head "no." She said, "I

am the Fishmonger. It's my job to clean fish."

"But I will help, if you'll let me," said Wordsmith.

Wordsmith stood up and put on a fish-cleaning apron and fish-cleaning gloves. She looked funny wearing Fishmonger's clothes. She picked up Fishmonger's knife and started cleaning the fish. She was not very good at it. She did not know how to use the knife well.

Fishmonger stood up. She said, "Here, let me show you."

Wordsmith handed the knife to Fishmonger, who showed her how to clean and prepare the fish.

Wordsmith said, "Fishmonger, you are very skilled at this."

"It only takes practice," said Fishmonger. "Anyone can learn to clean fish."

"Even a wordsmith?" said Wordsmith.

"Even a wordsmith," said Fishmonger.

"Even a bat scientist?" said Wordsmith.

Fishmonger smiled a little bit. Wordsmith saw that her friend was going to be okay. "Fishmonger," said Wordsmith, "we will clean the fish together. Then we will go outside together to enjoy the sunshine and the birds."

As they worked side by side, Fishmonger and Wordsmith talked about all the things they could do once they were done cleaning the fish.

They decided that they would go out to the far end of the garden, near the pond and the chickens. They would drink coffee at the small table under the tall pear trees and be exactly who they wanted to be: Bat Scientist and Great Poet, themselves, together.

Cake

Fishmonger stood in her kitchen wearing a stained apron printed with small fish. It had two very large, deep pockets where she sometimes slipped odd things she found about the house—a paper clip, an acorn, a small stone, a piece of blue Lego, and many Kleenexes.

The oven was on and she was sweating. The heat from the stove in her small kitchen added to what was already a hot sunny July day. But the sweat on her forehead didn't bother her. She was so, so pleased with what she had just pulled out of the oven. It smelled fabulous! Much better than smoked fish.

Atop the stove were two round pans of steaming, freshly baked chocolate cake. They filled the kitchen with such a sweet, rich aroma that Fishmonger felt giddy. It was going to be a magnificent, fabulous cake. As soon as the layers cooled, she would stack them, adding some buttercream icing and fresh strawberries in between.

Wordsmith would be arriving soon. The cake was perfect, and Fishmonger was excited to share it. It was a great pleasure to eat fresh cake in the company of a good friend.

Wordsmith arrived on her bicycle. She was very sweaty from the ride under the hot July sun.

Her face was flushed but she was happy to have pedalled all the way to Fishmonger's house.

Fishmonger poured two tall glasses of cold water with ice cubes, one for Wordsmith and one for herself. Wordsmith drank gratefully and looked refreshed.

Wordsmith sat at the kitchen table, next to the window with the bird feeder. The glasses of water sweated in the warm air, leaving puddling rings on the wood.

Fishmonger put two plates and two forks on the table. Then she brought over the cake.

"OOOOOOOOoooooooohhhhhhhhh!" said Wordsmith. She didn't have any words to say, only happy sounds.

Fishmonger smiled a big, satisfied smile.

Everything was as perfect as could be. Cake, Wordsmith and cold water. It was a beautiful day for enjoying some of her favourite things.

Fishmonger and Wordsmith admired the chocolate cake for some time. It was good to sit and drink cold water and look at the dessert awhile before tasting it.

"Wordsmith, would you like a piece of cake?" asked Fishmonger, "I made it myself."

Wordsmith nodded her head vigorously and said, "Fishmonger, a slice of your chocolate cake would be just the thing to make this day even more wonderful."

Fishmonger cut two thick slices with her filleting knife and put a big wedge on each plate.

The two friends ate thoughtfully and slowly, savouring each bite. The only sounds were "mmmmmmmmm" and "mmmmmhhhmmmmm." They took sips of water between forkfuls of cake.

Fishmonger and Wordsmith were content and relaxed. They slowly finished their slices. Then they picked at the moist crumbs on their plates. They sipped more water. They watched the birds at the feeder. They talked a little bit about their children and their husbands and about other parts of their lives.

And they looked at the cake.

Fishmonger said, "Wordsmith, the cake is so fresh, and I made it especially for you. Won't you have another piece?"

Wordsmith said, "Why thank you, Fishmonger! I don't mind if I do. But only if you'll have one with me."

"Oh, if you insist!" said Fishmonger. And she cut two more pieces of cake with her filleting knife.

The day went on, and the sun slowly crossed the sky. The heat became less and the shadows longer. A bit of a breeze came in through the open window. The two friends felt delightfully more comfortable and not so hot and sweaty. They sat at the table, talking and not talking, and eating the cake.

Wordsmith saw now that there was not very much cake left—only enough for two modest pieces. She said, "Oh, Fishmonger! We've eaten almost all of your delicious cake! You will have none left for tomorrow."

Wordsmith was alarmed and sad. It truly had been a large cake, and there was now so very little left. They had been enjoying each other's company and enjoying the taste and smell of the chocolate, but now, Wordsmith felt bad that her friend's beautiful cake was nearly all gone.

"Do not worry!" said Fishmonger. "I made it for you. It does not need to last. I would not want to eat it alone."

"In fact," she said, "let's finish it now. There's no one else I would want to eat a whole cake with."

They laughed in a way that was both happy and guilty—What an indulgence!—as they spooned the last of the cake greedily into their mouths, straight from the platter, and scraped up the crumbs.

They sat back in their seats, full and pleased, resting their hands on their bellies. They sighed. They were content.

But soon, Wordsmith felt that her waistband was too tight. She undid the top button of her pants. This helped, but she was still feeling uncomfortably full.

She rubbed her belly and said, "Ohhh, Fishmonger, this was maybe not such a good idea."

Fishmonger was beginning to look slightly green. She nodded. "You're right, Wordsmith. It is perhaps better not to eat a whole cake, even with a good friend." She rubbed her full belly and made an unhappy moaning sound.

The two friends felt sheepish and their physical discomfort grew. It seemed the best thing to ease their full bellies and digest would be to lie down on the floor.

They slowly moved off their chairs and lay down on the hardwood, among the crumbs, with their feet under the table and their

heads side by side in the middle of the kitchen.

"We're quite silly, aren't we, Fishmonger?"
asked Wordsmith.

Fishmonger made a quiet agreeing sound.
"My beeeelllllllyyyy…," she moaned.

"I'm sorry," said Wordsmith.

"I'm sorry, too," said Fishmonger.

"But there's no one I'd rather be silly with than
you," said Wordsmith.

"Me too," said Fishmonger.

And then, as the sun approached the horizon,
turning the sky beautiful bright colours—orange,
fuchsia and purple—the two silly,
happy friends closed their eyes and fell asleep.

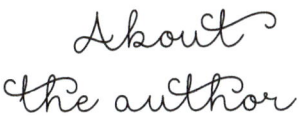

About
the author

Kristina Drake is an author, poet and editor living and

writing off the beaten path in Canada and Hungary.

Her chapbook *Ornithologies* was published by

above/ground press in 2017, and her poems have

appeared in *Carte Blanche* and *Soliloquies.*

www.kristinadrake.ca

More Stories

Enjoy more friendship stories and adventures

with Fishmonger and Wordsmith!

Seasons with Fishmonger and Wordsmith

Fishmonger and Wordsmith is a

Cat Creek publication.

catcreekcreations@gmail.com